CLAIRE and the DRAGONS

SCOUT COMICS

FB/TW/IG:
@scoutcomics

LEARN MORE AT:
www.scoutcomics.com

Brendan Deneen, *CEO*
James Haick III, *President*
Don Handfield, *CCO*
Lesa Miller, *COO*
Richard Rivera, *Exec. VP*
David Byrne, *Co-Publisher*
Charlie Stickney, *Co-Publisher*
Andrea Lorenzo Molinari, *Editorial Director*
Marcus Guillory, *Head of Design*
Trent Miller, *General Counsel*
Nicole D'Andria, *Director of Digital Content*

CLAIRE and the DRAGONS

VOLUME 1

CREATOR, WRITER, ARTIST
WANDER ANTUNES

TRANSLATION
MARJORY ABULEAC AND THATY MARIANA

SCOUT EDITOR
ANDREA LORENZO MOLINARI

SCOUT PRODUCTION
SEAN CALLAHAN

CHAPTER 1

ALL RIGHT, LET ME HANDLE THIS, GUYS! I'M GOOD WITH GIRLS. YOU KNOW THAT, RIGHT?

NOW...YOU HAVE MY FULL ATTENTION. THAT'S WHAT YOU WANT, ISN'T IT? IF I CHAT WITH YOU FOR A WHILE, WILL YOU STOP BOTHERING US? ALL WE WANT IS A WORD WITH--

CROOOU!

GO AWAY... LEAVE LONTAR ALONE, YOU SELF-ABSORBED JERKS!

YOU THINK YOU CAN TAKE US, GIRL?

UFF...

YEP... I DOOOO!

ARG!

TUM!

YOU'RE KIND OF SLOW HUH, KID?

CROOU!

AAAAHHHH!

LEAVING ALREADY? SMART MOVE.

SO, YOU LITTLE GUYS HAD ENOUGH? I EXPECT YOU HAVE.

YOU...YOU'RE GOING TO PAY FOR THIS! AAAAHHHH!

IF YOU'RE LOOKING FOR MORE ACHES AND PAINS, FEEL FREE TO COME TO DISTURB LONTAR AGAIN.

BUT IF YOU DO COME BACK... I'LL BE HERE WAITING FOR YOU, BOYS.

G-GO AWAY, PLEASE!

GO AWAY!

WOW! IT'S DOING WHAT I ASKED!

AAAAAH!

THAT THING...

AHHH...

IT'S GONE, MORONS! BUT SOMETHING TELLS ME IT'S GOING TO BE BACK.

THANK GOD YOU'RE HERE! I CAN'T IMAGINE WHAT WOULD'VE HAPPENED IF YOU HERO TYPES WEREN'T HERE.

I BET YOU GUYS EARN A GOOD LIVING PROTECTING LOCAL VILLAGES.

W-WE'RE GOING! WE'RE GONNA GET AS FAR AWAY FROM YOU AS WE CAN!

NAH! REALLY? THAT DOESN'T SURPRISE ME.

YEAH, BOYS, YOU'D BEST GET AS FAR AWAY FROM HERE AS YOUR STUBBY LEGS CAN CARRY YOU!

YEAH... GULP!

HEEELP!!

"POOR CLAIRE. FROM THIS MOMENT ONWARD, EVERYTHING IS GOING TO CHANGE.

"AND THIS IS JUST THE BEGINNING. THE DRAGONS ARE COMING, GIRL! AND YOU MUST FACE THEM.

"ARE YOU GOING TO FACE THEM...OR RUN AWAY?

"I'M NOT FACING THEM! DO YOU REALLY THINK IT'S EVEN POSSIBLE!"

CHAPTER 2

"YOU ARE NOT READY TO FIGHT YET. RUN!"

RRRROOOOOAARRRR!

"HURRY, MY CHILD, THE DRAGON IS GETTING CLOSER."

WHOOMP! WHOOMP!

THIS VOICE IN MY HEAD... LONTAR?

HELP!

HURRY!!

"IT'S ME INDEED, CLAIRE. THAT'S IT, GET INSIDE THAT HOLE, QUICK!!"

FUSHH!

ARG!

AHHH!

"SEE? THE DRAGON KNOWS YOU ARE THE ENEMY TO BE DEFEATED!

SSWISHHH!

THAT'S WHY IT'S FURIOUS!

GRRRRRR!!

IT DOESN'T KNOW WHERE WE ARE HIDING.

BUT WE'RE STUCK HERE NOW!

YEP!

WHAT ARE WE GOING TO DO?

WE CAN'T STAY...AND WE WONT!

WE'RE GOING OUT, BUT NOT THROUGH WHERE WE CAME FROM. COME!

THESE CAVES CUT THROUGH THE MOUNTAIN FROM ONE SIDE TO THE OTHER.

ALL OF THE MOUNTAINS. OR NEARLY ALL.

HOPEFULLY, WE'LL BE LUCKY TO--

--STAY AWAY FROM THE ABYSS, GIRLS!

LIGHT! THERE IS A WAY OUT...AHEAD.

IT APPEARS THAT WE'VE THROWN THE DRAGON OFF OUR TRAIL.

HOPEFULLY... HEY!

GRRRRRRRRR!

NO..IT'S OUT THERE...HOW DID IT KNOW?!

CALM DOWN.

HOW COULD IT?

OF COURSE--

--IT'S ME! LIKE LONTAR SAID...IT FEELS MY PRESENCE!

LET'S THINK ABOUT A WAY TO--

--CLAIRE... COME BACK HERE!

GO GET THE HERB!

I WILL KEEP THIS CREATURE BUSY!

GRRRRRRRR! WHOMP! WHOMP!

GRRRRRRRRRR!

IT'S COMING... WHAT DO I DO NOW?

"NOW YOU RUN, CLAIRE!

CHAPTER 3

THIS PLACE...

THE OBLIVION PIT-- DON'T YOU REMEMBER? WHAT DID YOU DO TO BE THROWN HERE?

OBLIVION PIT? THROWN? ME?! NO! I WAS RUNNING AWAY FROM...WELL, I FELL IN HERE! THAT'S IT, I FELL IN HERE!

THEY THROW CRIMINALS, ENEMIES OF THE POWERFUL IN HERE.

IT'S IMPOSSIBLE TO GET OUT OF HERE!

H-HOW SO? I NEED TO GET BACK UP THERE!

THE ONLY WAY OUT IS THROUGH THE WAY YOU CAME IN--BUT THAT'S WAY TOO HIGH! THERE IS NO WAY TO REACH. I'M VERY SORRY.

THERE MUST BE A WAY!

YOU'LL BE WELCOME IN MY CITY, WE ARE A PEACEFUL PEOPLE... IT'S NEAR HERE. CAN YOU WALK?

I THINK I CAN.

IT'S BAD ENOUGH THAT I HAVE TO SAVE THE WORLD FROM DRAGONS AND NOW I MUST--

DRAGONS?! WHAT... HEY!

SHH! DON'T SAY ANYTHING!

?

SEE! I DON'T THINK THERE WILL BE AN ATTACK TODAY.

RRRRRRRR!

WHAT DID YOU DO? THE COUNCIL WILL BE FURIOUS.

WHY? WE SAVED THE VILLAGE! LOOK HOW THEY ARE RUNNING AWAY.

THEY'LL THANK US.

THEY DON'T WANT TO MAKE THE THIEVES ANGRY...

...SPEAKING OF THE COUNCIL...

DON'T UPSET THE THIEVES...

...I CAN'T BELIEVE YOU SAID THAT!

WHAT WAS THAT NOISE? THIS GIRL IS NOT ONE OF US!

THEN CLAIRE CAUSED AN AVALANCHE AND--

SHE CREATED TROUBLE FOR OUR VILLAGE. THAT'S WHAT SHE DID!

TROUBLE? I SAVED YOU!

NOSY! WE DON'T FIGHT, YOUNG LADY. NEVER! WE RUN AWAY AND SURVIVE! YOU BROUGHT TROUBLE--STAY AWAY FROM OUR VILLAGE!

STAY AWAY? BUT WHERE AM I SUPPOSED TO GO?

I'M AFRAID I CAN'T TALK TO YOU ANYMORE...

* THEY CAN'T SEE LONTAR.

* THE HIGHEST MOUNTAIN IN THE WORLD (SEE PREVIOUS EPISODE).

WOW!

THEY ARE EVERYWHERE!

YEP! AS I SAID, THE GIRLS WORKED HARD.

AND THE PLACE WAS WELL CHOSEN. AT THE END, THERE IS A CAVE TOO SMALL FOR THE MONSTER TO ENTER, BUT PERFECT FOR US!

AH, ONE MORE THING...

?

...IF THE STAKES DO NOT STOP THE CREATURE, I'LL BE WAITING FOR IT WITH MY POISONED BOW AND ARROWS.

I HOPE YOU ARE A GOOD ARCHER.

VERY GOOD, BELIEVE ME!

WELL...I...I HAVE TO GET THE DRAGON'S ATTENTION, DON'T I?

IT FEELS YOUR PRESENCE, SO...

OKAY. I UNDERSTAND. I'LL STAY WHERE IT CAN SEE ME...

...BUT FIRST, A HUG?

A VERY TIGHT ONE!

GO GET HIM, CLAIRE... COURAGE!!

HIT HIM, ELZA!

JUST A CHILD... POOR GIRL!

PEOPLE AVOID THINKING ABOUT THE THINGS THAT TERRIFY THEM. AND THAT'S EXACTLY WHAT THEY TRIED TO DO WITH DRAGON ATTACK.

AS IT WASN'T POSSIBLE, THEY TRIED TO CONVINCE THEMSELVES THAT THE REPORTS WERE FANCIFUL.

A DRAGON? YES, I SAW IT TOO... I WAS DRUNK, OF COURSE!

POOR YOU, SO YOU SEE DRAGONS ALL THE TIME...

IT TOOK A WHILE, BUT THEN, AFTER SOME HARVESTS, DROUGHTS, AND FLOODS--AND KILLING AND DYING IN MANY BATTLES--THEY FORGOT ABOUT IT AND LIFE WENT ON--AS IT ALWAYS DOES.

HOWEVER, A WOMAN NAMED ELZA AND A GIRL NAMED CLAIRE HAVE NOT FORGOTTEN.

GREAT, CLAIRE!

TCHAC! TCHAAC! TCHAAC!

HOW ABOUT I TRAIN A LITTLE MORE?

ENOUGH FOR TODAY! GIVE ME THAT BOW RIGHT NOW!

I DON'T FEEL READY...

YOU ALREADY SHOOT MUCH BETTER THAN ME, CLAIRE.

BUT YOU CAN'T TRAIN ALL THE TIME, YOU NEED TO LEARN TO REST.

IT'S...THOSE THINGS...

YES, THEY WILL BE BACK, UNFORTUNATELY! AT SOME TIME AND PLACE... ANOTHER DRAGON! OR MANY, WHO KNOWS.

YOU SAID THAT PEOPLE DON'T BELIEVE.

SOME BECAUSE THEY ARE SCARED, OTHERS BECAUSE THEY HAVEN'T SEEN.

WE SAW AND WE KNOW. I WISH IT WASN'T TRUE.

BUT NOW WHAT I REALLY WANT IS TO SLEEP...GOOD NIGHT, ELZA!

GOOD NIGHT, CLAIRE!

YAAWN!

SO MUCH RESPONSIBILITY... A CHILD STILL...

SHE WILL DO WELL, DON'T WORRY!

...LONTAR!

COVER
GALLERY

CLAIRE & THE DRAGONS

THE

A comic book project by:
WANDER ANTUNES

COMICTOM101 · SCOUT COMICS

VARIANT